Rembrandt's Hat

Written by Susan Blackaby • *Illustrated by* Mary Newell DePalma

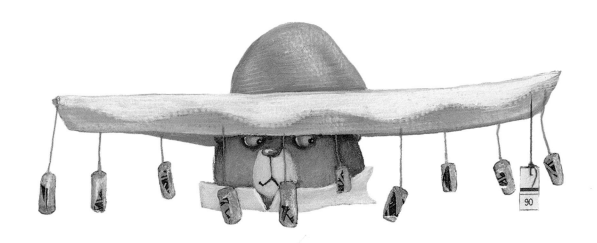

Houghton Mifflin Company
Boston 2002

In memory of Mif Blackaby
—S. B.
For Joe, Bill, and Dan
—M. N. D.

Text copyright © 2002 by Susan Blackaby
Illustrations copyright © 2002 by Mary Newell DePalma

www.houghtonmifflinbooks.com

The text of this book is set in 15-point Cheltenham.
The illustrations are mixed media.

Library of Congress Cataloging-in-Publication Data

Blackaby, Susan.
Rembrandt's hat / by Susan Blackaby ; illustrated by Mary Newell DePalma.
p.   cm.
Summary: When Rembrandt the bear loses his special lucky hat, he finds that
neither a bird, nor a cat, nor a clown hat can replace it.
ISBN 0-618-11452-1
[1. Hats—Fiction. 2. Lost and found possessions—Fiction. 3. Bears—Fiction.]
I. DePalma, Mary Newell, ill. II. Title.
PZ7.B5318 Re 2002   [Fic]—dc21   2001030881

Printed in Singapore
TWP 10 9 8 7 6 5 4 3 2 1

On what began as a fine day,
a bear named Rembrandt lost his hat.

He had stopped in the park to watch a clown juggle eggs, and while he was watching, a gust of wind snagged the tip of his hat and carried it away, just like that.

"Oh, no!" said Rembrandt, grabbing at sky. "Oh, please! Come back!"

Rembrandt hurried after the breeze. He saw something splash down into a puddle, but it wasn't his hat.

It was a bird.

"What's up?" asked the bird.

"I thought you were my lucky hat," said Rembrandt. "I lost it."

"Doesn't sound very lucky." The bird kicked up a muddy fizz.

"Maybe you saw it," said Rembrandt. "It was a comfortable, everyday sort of hat. It was just your color."

"By golly, I think I did," said the bird.

"Really? Which way did it go?"

"Up and over and then up again and then gone," said the bird.

"Oh," said Rembrandt, touching his ear. "Oh," he said, sighing.

"Cheer up!" said the bird. "I'll be your hat." He hopped onto Rembrandt's head. "How's that?" he called.

The bird's wet little feet felt prickly.

"OK," said Rembrandt. "Fine."

"Well, carry on," said the bird.

Rembrandt tried, but it was hard.

The bird could arrange his wings and tail to be any sort of hat, but he couldn't hold a pose for very long.

"Cramp!" he'd call.

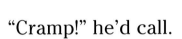

Then he would hop around on Rembrandt's head and settle back down in a completely different style.

One day, as Rembrandt listened to
the bird complain about a cat that had
been following them, he noticed the cat
peeking out from behind a tree.

"Are you *sure* he's following us?"
whispered Rembrandt. "Maybe we all just happen to be here.
Maybe we're following *him* without even knowing it."

"Oh, please." The bird hopped to his feet. "I know when I'm
being followed."

The cat stepped into the path. He bowed. "Your hat looks good
enough to eat," he said in a hoarse whisper.

"Thank you," said Rembrandt.

"Get lost, fuzz face!" snapped the bird.

"He's a plump little hat, isn't he," said the cat.

"That's it," said the bird. "I'm out of here." He launched himself
into the air and spiraled upward.

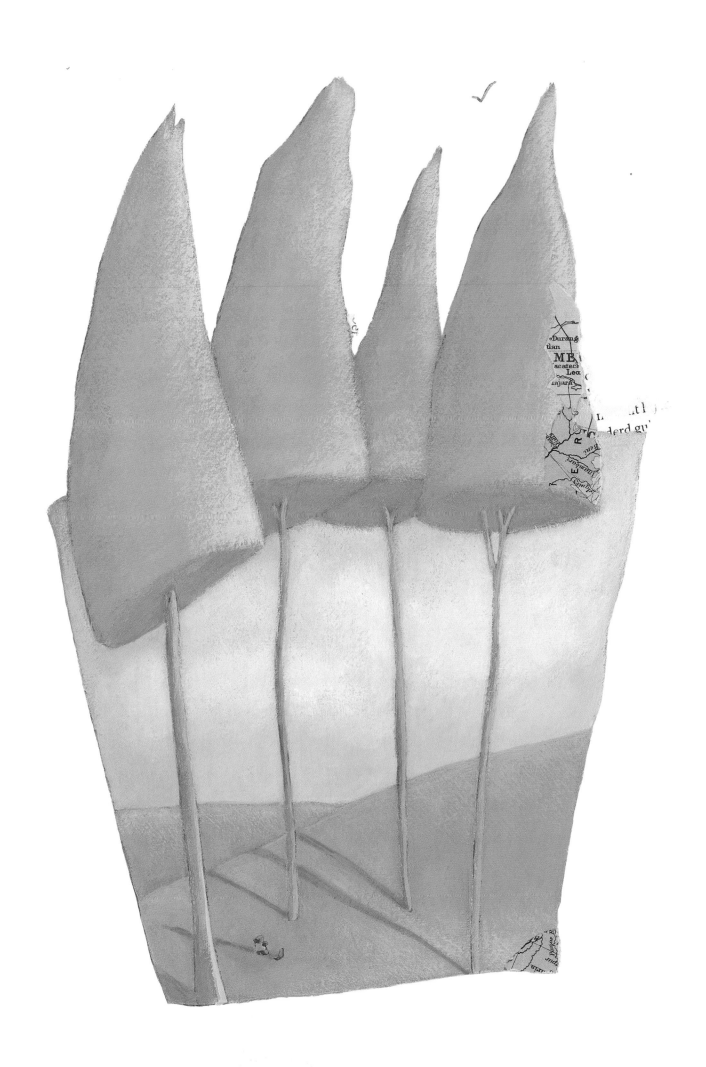

Rembrandt and the cat watched the bird disappear.

Rembrandt sighed. "That's two hats lost."

"I feel partly responsible," said the cat. "Oh, well. Never mind. I'll be your hat." He climbed onto Rembrandt's head. "You may call me Boo."

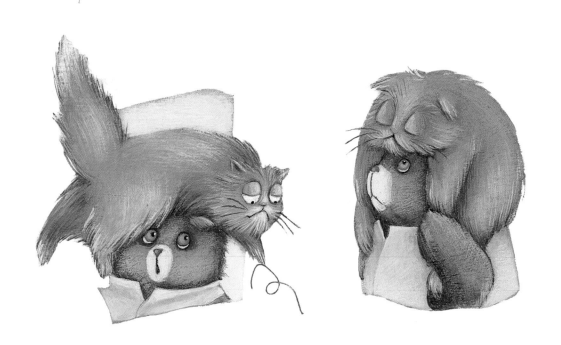

For a hat, Boo was heavy and lumpy. He gave Rembrandt a stiff neck. And Boo was easily distracted.

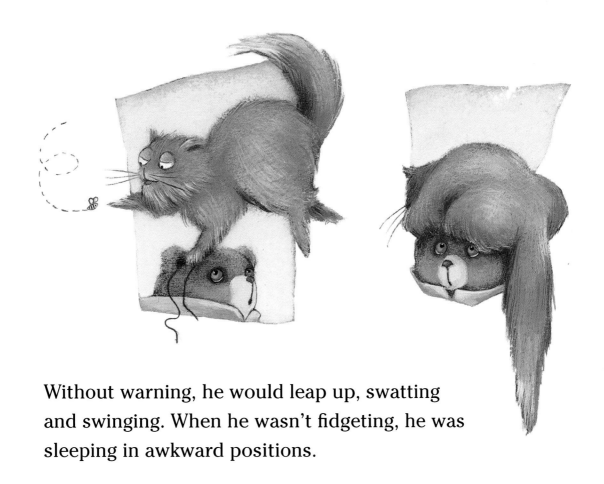

Without warning, he would leap up, swatting and swinging. When he wasn't fidgeting, he was sleeping in awkward positions.

Rembrandt tried to be patient.

One day, as Rembrandt trudged along, he was stopped by a rabbit wearing a fez.

"Excuse me," said the rabbit. "You have a cat sleeping on your head."

"I know." Rembrandt struggled to keep Boo from sliding sideways. "His name is Boo. He is sort of like a hat."

The rabbit looked puzzled.

"I had a real hat once," said Rembrandt. "It was my lucky hat."

"Well, you can't go around with a cat on your head," said the rabbit. "Never mind. I know what you need."

Rembrandt imagined having a rabbit for a hat. It could work.

The rabbit pointed right at Rembrandt's nose. "You need a hat shop," he said.

A hat shop!

Boo suddenly woke up. "Did I miss anything?" He blinked. "Who are you?"

"I'm Tip," said the rabbit.

"We're going to a hat shop!" said Rembrandt.

"A hat shop," said Boo. "Now there's an idea."

A little bell jingled as they entered the shop.

"My stars!" said Boo. "Every style for any occasion!" He tried on an elegant fedora. "These toppers are tops!"

"Look at this one," said Rembrandt, reaching up. "What do you think?"

"Too boring," said Boo. "You want something with a plume."

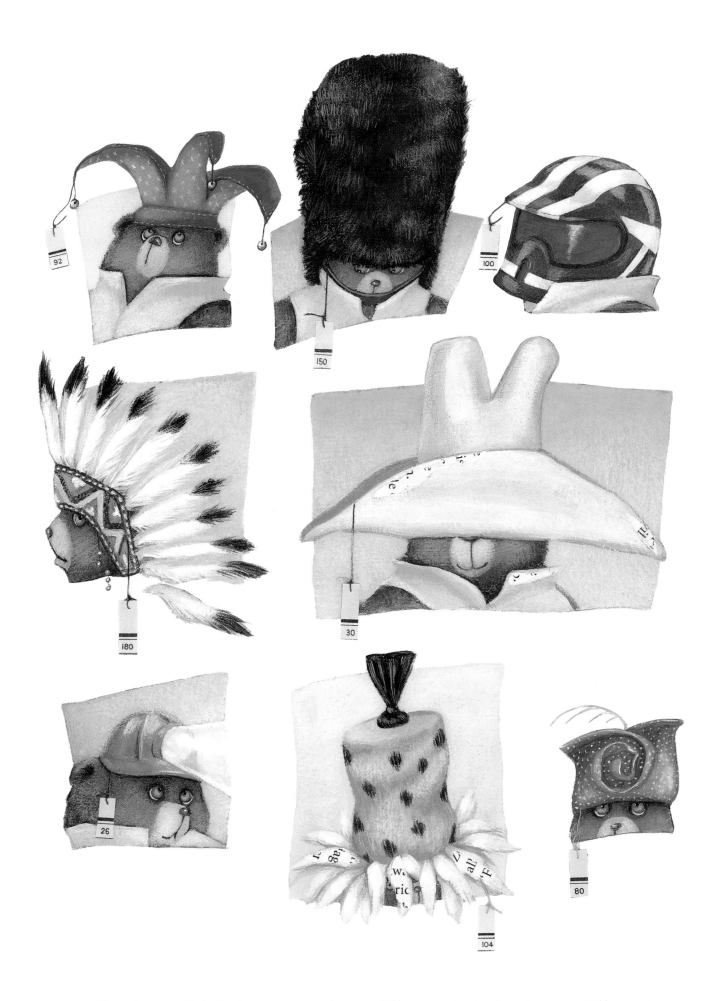

Rembrandt tried on seventeen different hats in eleven different colors. All of them were fantastic. None was quite right.

By now Boo and Tip were losing interest.

Tip waved at a clown hat. "Try that one," he said.

Rembrandt put it on.

"Perfect!" cried Tip, jumping up.

"Really?" Rembrandt looked in the mirror.

"Trust me," Tip said. "Look! It has chin ribbons."

Tip tied the hat on tight. "Let's go."

Boo yawned. He squinted at the pom-poms bobbing on top of the clown hat. "That's a fun touch," he said.

"Are you sure this hat is the one?" Rembrandt asked. "It seems so silly."

"Well, of course it does," said Tip, giving Rembrandt a little push. "It's you. Let's go."

"He's right. It's you," said Boo. "Sold!"

So Rembrandt paid for the hat, and they left the shop.

Rembrandt tried different ways
to wear the hat. He tucked his ears
in; he kept them out.

He tied the ribbons;
he let them flutter behind him.

He set the hat at one angle and then another.

He put it on frontward and backward.

Finally, he took the hat to the clown in the park.

"Would you like to have this?" he asked.

"Would I!" The clown popped the hat onto her head. "But what about you?"

"I think I can find what I want on my own," said Rembrandt. "I know exactly what I'm *not* looking for."

The clown winked and pulled a penny out of Rembrandt's ear. "Good luck," she said.

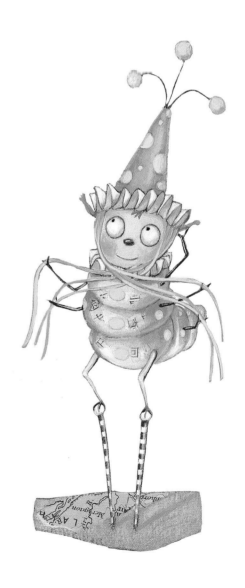

For the next few weeks, Rembrandt went about his business. He had almost—but not quite—forgotten about his lost hat until one day, as he was passing the souvenir stand near the baseball diamond, something familiar caught his eye.

It was a comfortable, everyday sort of hat in just the right color. Better still it had the right swirly letter stitched on the front.

Rembrandt pulled the hat down snug.

"Hey!" came a call from overhead. The bird glided down and hopped to a stop. "You found your lucky hat!"

Rembrandt nodded happily. "My *new* lucky hat," he said.